Walt Disney's

MORE TALES FROM THE MAGIC KINGDOM

BRIMAR

TWIN BOOKS

CONTENTS

BAMBI

There was great excitement in the forest. Friend Owl, who was sleeping peacefully, was awakened by the sound of voices. He leaned over, surprised, and discovered a beautiful sight. A newborn fawn was huddling against his mother, staring in astonishment at the crowd that surrounded him. Since early that morning, Thumper the rabbit had been announcing the good news. "Come quickly! A little prince is born!" And the forest animals had come from near and far to admire him.

In the company of his new friends, Bambi set out to explore the clearing, the forest, and the world. At first he had a little trouble standing up. It wasn't easy with legs as long as his! But with Thumper's advice and encouragement, he was soon gamboling everywhere. Thumper was proud to teach him what he knew.

"These are ferns, Bambi. We can hide under them. It's lots of fun." But the fawn had spotted something much prettier. "Oh! That's a butterfly," Thumper explained.

"But-but-butterfly!" Bambi repeated, watching in amazement as it flew away.

Thumper played the teacher. "Can you tell me what this is?" he asked, coming up to a bed of flowers.

"Butterfly?" Bambi answered shyly.

"Not quite — they're flowers!" laughed Thumper.

Just then, a little skunk popped out in front of them. "Flower?" said Bambi in wonderment.

Thumper was about to correct Bambi when the skunk spoke up. "That's okay," he said shyly. "He can call me Flower, if he wants to."

Bambi was very happy in the forest. Soon he learned to venture out. His mother taught him about many things: what plants could be eaten, places where water would always be found, and all about Man. The little fawn listened attentively. He asked all sorts of questions. But soon he'd had enough. Not far away was something very interesting.

It was a pool! Bambi leaned over, brought his muzzle to the water's surface, then backed up in bewilderment. Another fawn was doing exactly what he did! "It's only your reflection!" his amused mother explained. "But can you tell me what that is?"

Nearby, Bambi saw another reflection. But this time he ran and hid behind his mother. "Don't be scared, Bambi," she said, smiling. "Here is a friend for you. Her name is Faline."

Bambi was really happy to have Faline as a friend. Suddenly, however, right in the middle of their play, the whole forest seemed to be rushing past them. They were jostled and knocked about, as rabbits scampered between their legs. Faline fled, but Bambi, frozen by fear, couldn't move. Then a herd of stags arrived, and his mother rushed over, crying, "Quick, Bambi! Follow us. Man is in the forest!"

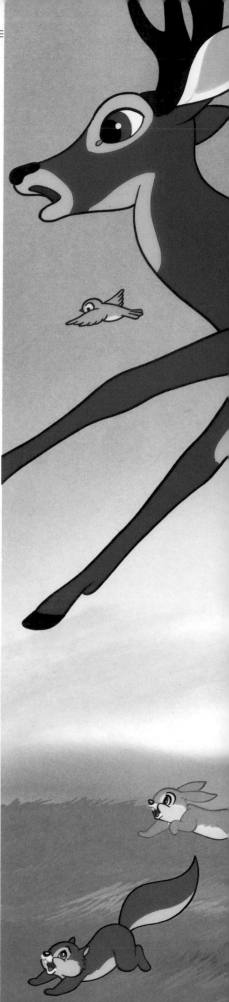

The deer took refuge in the deepest part of the forest, where they were safe. "When there is danger, you must come and hide here," explained Bambi's mother.

"The hunters won't come this way?" Bambi asked.

"No, it's too far for them. And more importantly, it's your father's territory. He will protect you." Just then, a magnificent stag came silently out from the shadows. "I am your father, Bambi, the Great Prince of the forest. One day, when you are grown, you will take my place." The little fawn was too impressed to speak.

That morning, the cold had awakened Bambi. A thick white blanket covered the ground. The little fawn was so surprised he stood for a moment without moving. "It's beautiful!" he cried. He set off running to warm himself up and — boom — fell down.

"Bambi, there's a trick to sliding on ice. You should have waited for me to show you." Thumper said, laughing. Then he helped Bambi to get up.

Snow continued to fall. It covered everything, and soon it became difficult to find plants to eat. "Mother, I'm cold and hungry!" Bambi complained.

Bambi's mother taught him to gnaw the bark of trees and dig up roots to satisfy his hunger. "Be patient, Bambi," she consoled him. "Spring will come again." But suddenly, she froze. Gunfire rang out in the mist. "Man! The hunters are coming! Run Bambi! Run and hide!"

Bambi ran without turning around. Terrified and out of breath, he finally stopped, looked back, and called his mother. But she wasn't there behind him. He was alone! Bambi began to cry. "Mother, where are you?" I'm lost!" Gusts of snow blew around him.

Suddenly Bambi was startled to hear someone approaching. The great stag came up beside him. "Courage, my son," his father said. "The hunters have taken your mother. But don't cry. From now on, I will look after you."

The days passed, and Bambi began to forget his sorrow. By the time spring came again, he had grown into a magnificent young stag. One morning, he met his friend, Thumper. He, too, had grown, and a beautiful female rabbit was with him. Flower the skunk had also found a mate. Bambi wanted to play, but his friends were too busy.

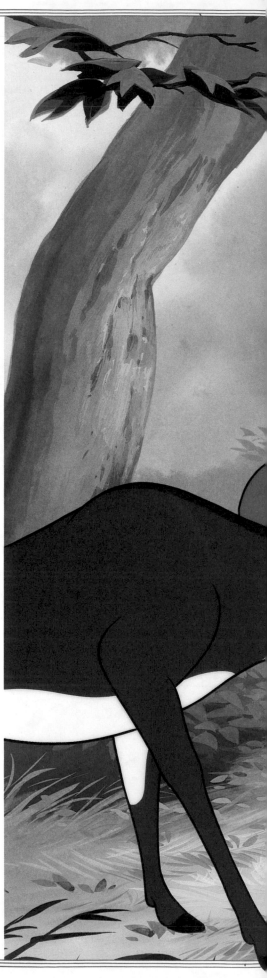

Just then, a familiar voice startled him. "What's the matter, Bambi. Don't you recognize me?" It was Faline! Bambi felt shy because she had become so beautiful!

"Come and walk with me," invited Faline. But suddenly, a fierce young stag named Ronno burst out of the thicket. "That doe is mine! Get out of here!"

Bambi realized that if he wanted to stay with Faline, he would have to fight.

Faline protested. She didn't want to go with Ronno. But Bambi's rival was already preparing to attack. The two young bucks glared at each other, backed up, gathered speed and hurled themselves forward. Their antlers clashed violently. Bambi was first to free himself and charge again. Ronno, caught off balance, staggered and fell. Then he got up and ran away. Bambi had won! Worried, Faline came up to him. "Are you all right, Bambi?" He nodded, and they looked tenderly at each other, knowing that nothing could separate them now.

Joining his father on a hilltop, Bambi told him of the fight and how he felt about Faline. "I'm proud of you," said the Great Prince of the forest. Then a strange odor filled the air around them, and they looked below. Some hunters had forgotten to put out their fire!

The fire spread rapidly, until the forest was transformed into a gigantic furnace. The animals tried to escape the flames and reach safety. But wherever they went, fire blocked their path. Flaming branches cracked and fell. It was hard to breathe because of the smoke. Bambi ran as fast as he could, but he was still exhausted from his recent battle. "Go on without me," he told his father. "I can't make it!"

"Courage, my son, keep going. We're almost there."

At last they reached water, but they still had to cross it. On the opposite bank the other animals watched the approaching fire. What a relief it was when Bambi and his father joined them, safe and sound! Happiest of all was Faline. "Bambi, you're safe!" she cried. "I was so afraid."

The great stag looked at them fondly. "I'm growing old," he said. "It's time for me to rest. It is Bambi's turn now to be the Great Prince of the Forest."

Bambi had taken his father's place. He proved worthy of the task that had been passed on to him and protected those around him. He and Faline were very happy together. And the following spring, the faithful Thumper announced the news: Bambi was a father!

In a sheltered clearing, Faline had brought not only one, but two lovely fawns into the world. All the animals of the forest gathered to admire them! Proudly, Bambi climbed to a rocky height above the trees and looked over his domain. His father would be pleased.

SLEEPING BEAUTY

"Phillip, this beautiful princess is named Aurora. One day you will marry her!" said King Hubert to his son.

But the young prince wasn't interested in the baby his father pointed out. He wanted to dance. His neighbor, King Stefan, was giving a splendid ball to celebrate their newborn daughter. Everyone from far and wide was invited. But it couldn't start until the godmothers arrived. And here they were, the three good fairies.

The fairies leaned over the cradle. "You shall be beautiful," said the first.

"And wise," said the second. But before the third could speak, there was a thunderclap and the evil fairy Maleficent appeared. "I was not invited," she said, "but I still have something to say. Beautiful and wise you shall be, but on your sixteenth birthday, you shall prick your finger on the spindle of a spinning wheel and die!"

The queen ran and took her baby in her arms, horrified. How would they protect the princess?

"Don't cry. I'm still here, and I have one wish left!" said the third fairy, waving her wand. "On your sixteenth birthday, if you prick your finger, you shall not die, but fall asleep. Only the kiss of a prince shall wake you."

To keep Aurora from the witch's evil spell, the king and queen entrusted her to the three fairies. They would call her Briar Rose, and raise her hidden in the forest, and Maleficent would never find her.

The years passed. Briar Rose grew into a beautiful, wise young girl. She didn't know that she was a princess, or that her godmothers were fairies. They decided never to use their magic powers, so that Maleficent could never find them.

And then one day, it was Briar Rose's sixteenth birthday. The fairies prepared a marvelous surprise: a lovely dress and a delicious cake.

"Go take a walk," they said. "We'll call you when everything's ready!"

After walking for a long time, Briar Rose sat down to rest. She leaned against the trunk of an oak tree and sang a song. Her voice was so pretty that all the animals came to listen: "One day a prince will come, and he'll carry me to his palace and we'll marry ..."

"If only I were that prince!" murmured a passing horseman who heard her song. He had never seen such a beautiful girl.

The birds joined in the chorus. And the young man dismounted, took Briar Rose in his arms, and twirled her into a dance. Alas, he should never have stopped dancing!

When he tried to ask her who she was, and if he could see her again, without answering, she ran away! The fairies had always told her never to talk to strangers.

During this time, the fairies were wrapping Briar Rose's presents. To make things go quickly, they decided to use their magic wands: presto, a dress and a cake! But the fairies didn't agree.

"The dress should be pink!" said one.

"No, blue!" said another, waving her hand in turn. And magic sparks went up the chimney! A raven sent as a spy by Maleficent, saw the colorful sparks and flew to tell her: the princess was alive!

When Briar Rose returned, she found the gifts her godmothers had wrapped. "Oh, thank you!" she cried. "What delicious cake, and what a beautiful dress ... I'll wear it for him!"

For him? The fairies were stunned. Then Briar Rose told them about her dance with the horseman, who wanted to see her again, even to marry her.

"That's impossible!" cried her godmothers. And they told Briar Rose the truth: she was the Princess Aurora, daughter of King Stefan, promised to Prince Phillip. They also told her about the evil spell. "But now," they added, "you're sixteen years old, and Maleficent has forgotten you. So we shall take you back home."

Aurora followed them sadly; she was thinking about the handsome young man whom she would surely never see again.

Soon they arrived at the castle. The fairies whisked her up to her room and helped her dress: "When you see your parents, you must be at your most beautiful! Now, don't move. We'll tell them you're here; it will be a wonderful surprise!"

But the fairies shouldn't have left the princess alone. The moment they left, a mysterious wisp of light appeared. As if in a trance, Aurora rose and followed it up a dark stairway.

At the top of the stairway was an attic. And in it was a spinning wheel. Who could have put it there? Long ago, to protect their daughter, the king and queen had banned them from the kingdom.

An irresistible force lifted Aurora's arm. Her finger came to rest on the spindle, and was pricked by the sharp point. The princess fell to the floor.

A shadow appeared beside her: Maleficent! "You thought you could escape! But no one can resist my powers!"

Finding Aurora's room deserted, the fairies guessed what had happened. Sadly, they found the princess in the attic and laid her out on her bed. Her poor parents had rejoiced so at her return. But perhaps they need not know!

The fairies decided to plunge the whole castle into a deep sleep. As long as Aurora slept, no one else would awaken.

Meanwhile, in Maleficent's palace, Aurora's horseman had been chained up. He was, in fact, Prince Phillip, now the witch's prisoner. "So, you will never save your love," mocked Maleficent. "The girl you met in the forest is your betrothed. But my evil spell has taken effect, and you will not escape."

However, Maleficent hadn't counted on the three good fairies. After a long search, they found the prince, and while the witch was away, they freed him. They had brought a magic shield and sword.

Phillip escaped from Maleficent's palace and galloped full-speed toward Aurora's home. The witch returned to find him gone.

But Maleficent wasn't admitting defeat. She transformed herself into a terrible dragon, flew through the air and appeared before the frightened prince. "You thought you could best me," she cried, "but you haven't won yet!" The foul beast, spitting white-hot flames, barred the way to the castle. How could Phillip get by her?

Although he fought bravely, the prince was forced to retreat to the edge of a ravine. If he backed up any farther, he would fall; if he went forward, the dragon would devour him. In desperation, Phillip threw the magic sword. It lodged in the heart of the beast, killing Maleficent.

The prince raced into the sleeping castle and found his love. Leaning over Aurora, he gave her a kiss.

Aurora opened her eyes and recognized her horseman. "I am Prince Phillip," he said, "the man you are to marry!"

Aurora smiled happily. They had finally found each other! At that moment, as the fairies had decreed, everyone in the castle, from basement to attic, awoke. The king and queen felt a little sleepy, but because of the magic spell they didn't remember anything.

The princess found her parents, and they wept with joy as they held their daughter in their arms. Soon after, Aurora and Phillip were married.

At their wedding ball, they danced all night. Aurora was beautiful in the gown created for her by the fairies: a splendid dress of blue ... no, pink ... no, blue! The fairies were arguing again. But under their protection, the lovers would live happily ever after!

THE ARISTOCATS

Madame Adelaide Bonfamille was a charming elderly lady who lived in Paris and was very rich. She lavished all her love on her cats, whom she considered the children she had never had. They were very wellbred, wellmannered cats. In the music room one day, Marie was singing, Berlioz was playing the piano, and Toulouse was painting pictures. Duchess, their mother, observed them lovingly. "Well done, my darlings," she purred.

Meanwhile, Madame Bonfamille was receiving her near-sighted attorney, a lifelong friend. "My dear Mr. Hautecourt," she said, "I want to make my will. Since I have no family, I shall leave everything to my beloved cats. I am sure that Edgar, my butler, will be glad to look after them when I pass away, he is so fond of them. And he will inherit my fortune when they are gone."

She did not know that Edgar, curious about the attorney's visit, had been listening to their conversation. Mr. Hautecourt agreed to everything. He kissed Duchess's tail instead of Madame's hand as he left.

Downstairs, Edgar was choking with anger. "It's outrageous," he thought, pacing back and forth in the kitchen. "I have served Madame faithfully all these years, and now she is going to leave her fortune to those beastly cats. And I am supposed to be butler to them! I won't have it!"

Suddenly, an evil glint lit up his eyes. "Ah-ha!" he exclaimed in glee, "I have it!" He added some sleeping pill to the cats' dinner, as he prepared it.

Duchess, Marie, Berlioz and Toulouse fell sound asleep. Edgar waited until night had fallen and Madame Bonfamille had gone to bed. Then the coast was clear for his wicked plan. "Sweet dreams, my precious little pets," he snickered as he seized the cats' basket.

Edgar drove into the country on his motorcycle with the basket in the sidecar. He was going to leave Duchess and her kittens so far from home they would never find their way back!

But when he came to the river, Edgar was attacked by two angry dogs. They chased him, barking and snapping at his legs. Trying to escape them, Edgar lost control of the motorcycle. The wayward machine ran away with him, skidding off the road. When it hit a bump, the basket flew out and rolled down the riverbank with its precious cargo. The terrified butler never noticed. He sped away without a glance behind him.

Luckily, the basket rolled to the edge of the river without falling in. The jolt had awakened the cats.

"Where are we? Why is it so cold and dark? What has happened to us?" they asked each other. To make matters worse, it began to rain.

In Paris, Madame Bonfamille was distraught to find that her cat and kittens had disappeared. Roquefort the mouse also searched the house from top to bottom. No doubt about it, they were gone!

Morning came at last. "Mama, we're hungry," whimpered the kittens. Duchess longed to comfort them but did not know how. "My poor children, I don't know how we got here, or how to get home, either."

At that moment, an enormous tawny alley cat appeared before her. "Hello, Princess," he said. "My name is O'Malley. Is there anything I can do for you?"

O'Malley did not have much polish, but he looked honest and helpful, so Duchess decided to trust him. She explained their predicament.

"I know how to get to Paris, and if you like, I'll take you home," said O'Malley. Duchess accepted at once.

To be sure of going in the right direction, they followed the railway tracks that led to the city. Suddenly, there was a terrifying noise: the train! They scurried to the bridge supports below the tracks, just in time.

Then Duchess let out a wail: "Marie has fallen into the river!" O'Malley dove off the bridge into the water. Desperately, he swam against the current and caught hold of the kitten, who was about to be swept away. He brought her back to shore.

"O'Malley, you have saved my daughter's life," said Duchess with tears in her eyes. "You are a hero!"

Fortunately, the rest of the journey was less eventful. Everything in the country was new to the kittens, and they loved it all: the trees, the flowers, the pebbles by the road, the people they met.

"Those two ladies smell so funny," whispered Berlioz to O'Malley.

O'Malley was amused. "That's because they're geese," he replied.

The kittens were soon very tired. It was a long way for them to walk on their little legs. "Will we soon be there?" they kept asking. It was nearly midnight when they reached Paris.

"I have an idea," said O'Malley. "I live close by with my friends the Scat Cats. Why don't you stay with us until tomorrow?" Duchess agreed at once, and they traveled over the rooftops to the house.

O'Malley's friends were great jazz musicians from all over the world. Duchess and her kittens danced the night away instead of resting.

"What a wonderful evening!" Duchess said softly to O'Malley. "I wish it would never end."

The kittens too were delighted. This was so much more fun than purring on a cushion. But in the morning, the time came to part. Madame Bonfamille would be very worried about them.

However, when they rang the doorbell it was Edgar who opened the door.

Quick as a flash, Edgar caught the cats in a sack before they knew what was happening. Luckily, Roquefort heard them mewing in distress. He ran this way and that, but there was only a big, sad-looking alley cat sitting outside the front door who might be able to help.

"Oh my," Roquefort thought with a shudder, "what if he tries to eat me?" He would have to risk it. He rushed out to O'Malley and talked so fast O'Malley could hardly grasp what he was saying. Then the big cat acted.

"I'll go find them," he said. "You go and get my friends."

"Say, how about this!" the Scat Cats jeered when they saw Roquefort. "Here's a mouse throwing himself into our paws." But as soon as Roquefort had explained his mission, they set out to help.

In the stables, Edgar dropped the sack with Duchess and the kittens inside into a big trunk. "You're going on a long voyage," he sniggered. "Soon you'll be far, far away, and the fortune will be all mine!" At that moment, O'Malley leapt onto his back with the fury of a wild beast.

Then the Scat Cats arrived and took over, clawing and biting Edgar. "Help! help! It's an army of devils attacking me," the butler yelled.

Meanwhile, O'Malley had gone to release the prisoners. Duchess looked at him gratefully. "What would I ever do without you?" she asked. "You're always there when we need you."

Scratched all over, Edgar tried to get away, but Madame Bonfamille's mare, Frou Frou, gave him a kick that sent him flying head-first into the trunk. When the movers came to pick it up, Edgar was inside, still out cold. So off he went on the long voyage he had planned for the cats. Good riddance!

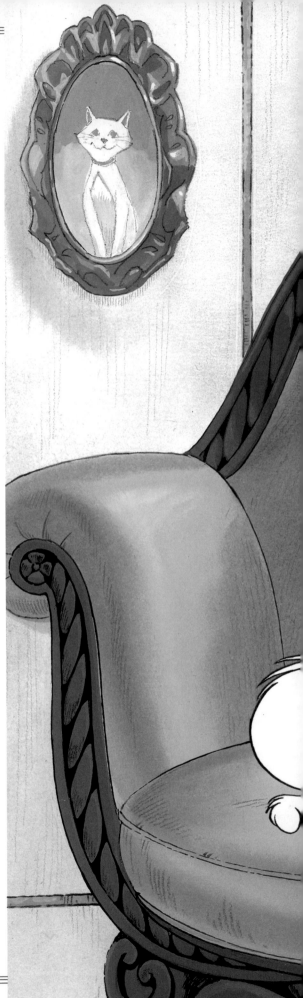

O'Malley hung back at the door to the elegant house, but Duchess urged him inside.

"I thought I had lost you for ever, my darlings," cried Madame Bonfamille, weeping with joy. "And you, big-hearted cat, come in, my house is yours. I'm going to adopt you, so put on this bow tie and pose with the others for a photograph."

"Hooray!" cried the kittens and Roquefort at once. But Duchess only looked at the beaming O'Malley and smiled.

THREE
LITTLE
PIGS

One day, three little pigs set out to make their way in the world. They decided to settle together beside a forest, but each wanted to build his own house in his own way. Fifer Pig, the youngest, was a lazy little pig. He decided to build a house of straw. The straw would be light and easy to gather, he thought. He soon finished his little yellow house and could start playing his fife again.

Fiddler, the second little pig, built his house of wood. It was a lot of work to gather all those branches and saw all those boards. Between blows of his hammer, Fiddler would take his violin and play a tune for encouragement. He found all the effort tiring and did his work carelessly. But he said, "I don't care if my house isn't very strong. I think it's a fine house."

Practical Pig, the eldest, built his house of brick. He worked hard because he liked to do a job properly. Sometimes Fiddler and Fifer, who had already finished their houses, would come to see how their brother was doing.

"Come on, Brother, come and play with us," they said. "It's tiring and difficult to do a job right," Practical replied, waving his trowel, "but my house is going to be the finest and certainly the strongest."

So the other two pigs went away to have fun.

A little later, Fiddler and Fifer came back. "Have you finished yet?" they called.

"No, I haven't finished. Stop bothering me!" snapped their brother.

What a grouch he was, they thought. And besides, he was so fond of giving them lectures.

"You don't give a thought to tomorrow. You only think of having fun," said Practical Pig. "You won't be so cocky when the Big Bad Wolf comes around. But I'll be safe in my brick house."

The two little pigs laughed at him. What a 'fraidy-cat he was! What a lot of trouble over a wolf who might not even be real! They laughed and laughed as they skipped away singing, "Who's afraid of the Big Bad Wolf? Not us, not us, not us!"

"Suddenly, there was a horrible sound of snapping jaws. The wolf had come out of the woods!

"Mmmm, two plump little pigs," he gloated, his mouth watering. And he pounced at the foolish pair, who ran away squealing, each to his own house.

Fifer ran to his house of straw and bolted the door. Safe! But the wolf had made up his mind to capture him. He prowled round the house calling, "Come out, little pig! Or I'll huff, and I'll puff, and I'll blow your house down!"

Shaking with fright, Fifer braced himself and waited. The wolf huffed and puffed so hard that the straw blew away and the house scattered in the wind.

The Big Bad Wolf had blown Fifer's house down in no time! Squealing in terror, the little pig ran away, the wolf in hot pursuit.

Breathless, Fifer ran to Fiddler, saying, "Quick, into your house! The Big Bad Wolf is after me!" With chattering teeth, they slammed the door behind them. But the wolf was hatching a plan. He would disguise himself as a sheep. He licked his chops as he pictured the scrumptious meal awaiting him.

"O-o-open the do-or", bleated the wolf pitifully. "I'm a poor little l-l-lost l-l-lamb."

But Fiddler and Fifer recognized the voice. "We know who you are, and we won't open the door!" they said.

"Come out, little pigs!" called the wolf. "Or I'll huff, and I'll puff, and I'll blow your house down." And he took a deep breath.

"You can huff and puff all you want," replied the little pigs, who felt braver now. "Our house is made of wood this time, and you can't blow it down."

But the wolf huffed and puffed so hard and so long that the boards separated and the roof blew off. Only the door stood firm. Frightened out of their wits, the little pigs ran and ran. The ravenous wolf ran after them.

The two frantic little pigs reached Practical's house
just in time.

"Don't panic," said their brother as he let them in.
"My house is made of brick strong and well built, so
we'll all three be safe."

Fiddler and Fifer hid under the bed, still shaking.
They had a hard time believing that they were safe
from the Big Bad Wolf. They could hear him gnashing
his teeth outside, furious not to have caught them.
What would he think up now to trick them?

"Three little pigs all at once," said the wolf to himself. "What a feast!" He was hatching a new plot. This time he came disguised as a door-to-door salesman. "Open the door," he said in a quavering voice. "Toothbrushes, shoebrushes, hairbrushes, all kinds of brushes for sale."

But Practical Pig was not fooled. "Take that!" he cried, giving the wolf's hairy foot in the door a wallop with his own brush. Try as he might, the wolf could not get in.

Finally, the wolf lost his temper and began to huff and puff... so hard he lost his pants, which made the little pigs laugh. He huffed and puffed some more. Not a shingle on the house budged.

What would the disappointed wolf do now? "I want those three plump litle pigs for my supper," he groaned. "The house is too strong, the door is too secure and the little pigs are too cautious. Ah-ha! I know — I'll get in by the chimney." The wolf crept onto the roof, but Practical Pig knew what he was up to. He had a trick to play on the Big Bad Wolf.

When the wolf slipped down the chimney — plop — he fell right into a big cauldron of hot water and smelly turpentine.

"Yeeow!" yelled the wolf. With his tail steaming, he shot out of the house like a rocket, headed for safety at the far end of the forest.

The three little pigs were saved!

The wolf wasn't likely to be back, and now the three little pigs could dance and sing to their heart's content in their safe little, snug little house: "Who's afraid of the Big Bad Wolf? Not us, not us, not us!"

FAT

MOTHER

THE
UGLY
DUCKLING

"The time has come, my dear. Our babies are ready to hatch." Mother Duck was tired from sitting on her eggs for so long, and Father Duck was a little concerned. He hoped everything would go well.

Tap! tap! Faint noises could be heard. The eggshells were cracking. And out they came, all yellow and downy. What a pretty sight! This batch had turned out particularly well and their parents were proud and happy.

But here was something strange: one egg hadn't hatched! It was the same color as the others, but it was much bigger. Father Duck leaned over to listen. Nothing was moving inside. What was he up to, the lazy little one? He was certainly in no hurry. At last the shell began to crack, and he stepped out. "But what is this?" asked Mother Duck, alarmed. "I've never seen a duckling like this one!" Indeed, the little duckling was white and really very large.

"Come, children, hurry up. It's bath time. You, back there, stop lagging behind. I'm in a hurry!" Mother Duck thought the big duckling was ugly and quite clumsy. She hoped at least he'd know how to swim.

They arrived at the water's edge.
"Come on, all of you. Climb up on my
back."

The big white duckling was last in
line. There wasn't much space, so he sat
behind his brothers on his mother's tail.
For this first trip on the river, Mother
Duck started off slowly, but soon she
picked up speed. The ugly duckling lost
his balance, flew through the air and fell
down behind her.

When he tried to catch up, his mother stopped and shouted at him, "Not only are you ugly, but you're clumsy. We won't have anything more to do with you." Pushing him with her bill, she left him in the water.

The other ducklings, annoyed that their outing had been interrupted, poked fun at him rudely. "You're too big! You're too white! You're not beautiful!" Then they went off without a backward glance.

The bewildered duckling sat down for a moment and didn't move. "Why are they treating me this way?" he wondered. "I've done nothing to hurt them!" Then he got up, leaned over the water and saw his reflection. He had thought he was like the other ducklings. Now he discovered he wasn't. He looked awful. He knew his mother and brothers would never accept him as he was.

"What will become of me?" wondered the little duck. "My own family doesn't want me!" He walked sadly along without really knowing where his feet were taking him.

A short while later, he was overcome by a strange feeling. He was hungry! But he was too little to feed himself. Who would give him something to eat? Just then, directly above his head, he heard: "Chirp, chirp, chirp."

Baby birds in a nest! They seemed pleased to have the duckling join them. "Our mother will come back soon," they said. "She went to find something for us to eat." The duckling, who was becoming hungrier and hungrier, was very happy with the way things were turning out.

A moment later, the mother bird returned with a big earthworm. The duck opened his bill expectantly.

But the bird wasn't pleased that a stranger had come into her nest without asking. "What are you doing here?" she demanded. You want to steal food from my children? Go away!"

The terrified duck jumped out of the nest, but the bird chased him, pecking at him with her beak.

The little duck threw himself into a pool, putting an end to the chase. Trembling and hiding beneath a water lily, he waited for the bird to go away. Having heard nothing for a while, he poked out his head and saw a gigantic, smiling duck.

At last, he'd found someone friendly. How marvelous! The duckling approached shyly. "Tell me, can we be friends?"

The big duck did not answer, but the smile remained on its face. Even if he wasn't a talker, he certainly seemed nice. The duckling was enchanted with his new friend and decided to play with him. He climbed on his back and on his beak. The giant was very patient, letting him do as he pleased without protest. But when the little duck swam up beside him, he bent over abruptly and whacked him on the head!

"What was that for? Doesn't he want to play with me anymore?" The duckling was unhappy, wondering why his big playmate was displeased. He watched him turn and float away, swaying from side to side. All this time he hadn't understood that he was playing with a wooden duck. That was why his friend never answered.

Another disappointment! The ugly duckling still
had no friends and no one to look after him.
The poor thing wandered for a bit along the
road, then returned to the edge of the pond. He
began to cry, not knowing what else to do.

As no one came to help him, the ugly duckling cried harder. You could hear him all over the pond. But suddenly, a soft voice asked: "What is this all about, my little one? What's the matter?"

The duckling was speechless as he stared at the splendid white bird who spoke to him so kindly.

"Stop crying and come play with us!" called four large white ducklings cheerfully. The ugly duckling joined them with delight.

After they had played for a while, the little duckling opened his heart to the big white mother bird. He told her all his troubles and asked, "Why do you, who are so beautiful, accept me? I'm ugly and no one loves me."

"That isn't so," the beautiful bird answered. "You were hatched in the wrong nest. I am a swan, and so are you! Look at yourself in the water. You're like my babies, and one day, you'll be just as beautiful as I am." Overjoyed, the ugly duckling was adopted into the swan family.

THE BRAVE LITTLE TAILOR

One morning, a wave of fear swept over a little town that was usually peaceful and secure. "The Giant is coming to town! Let's get away from here!" No one felt capable of facing the monster who had already destroyed half the country. Meanwhile, sounds of a scuffle could be heard in the workshop of the little tailor, whose name was Mickey: "Take that, and that!" *Pow! Pow! Pow!*

"Seven! I killed seven with one blow!" shouted the little tailor, pleased to be rid of the flies that were pestering him. His neighbors rushed over. The little tailor described his conquest again and again. "I killed seven at the same time, just like that! Pow!"

In no time the rumor reached the palace. "The tailor killed seven men with a single blow! He could get rid of the Giant for us!"

Eventually, the news came to the king. "Sire, it is said that the tailor killed seven men with one blow." The king ordered the worthy subject to be brought before him. "Since you are so brave," he said when the little tailor arrived, "you shall rid us of the Giant."

"M-me, Your Majesty?" the little tailor stammered. "But I ..."

"If you return alive," added the king, "you shall marry my daughter."

The little tailor's fears of confronting the Giant evaporated when he heard these words. The princess was so beautiful. What was more, she seemed to like him.

"Do not worry, Your Majesty. By tomorrow, he will be forgotten. I know exactly how to get rid of him," said the tailor, brandishing his scissors. The princess stepped from her throne and gave the brave tailor half a dozen kisses.

The little tailor left the palace at once with a determined stride. Once he stepped out the door, however, he slowed down a little. The princess waved at her new fiancé from her balcony. "Come back quickly. I have faith in you!" Her words pleased the little tailor, but he already regretted not having told the king the truth: It wasn't seven men he had killed; it was only seven flies.

The little tailor walked for hours through the countryside. There was no trace of the Giant nor any sign he'd been that way. Mickey had no idea where else to look and didn't dare return to the palace.

Exhausted, he sat down to rest for a moment. "And what if I *do* meet him?" he sighed worriedly. "He'll make mincemeat out of me!"

Just then, a gigantic shadow spread across the fields.

Boom! Boom! Boom! Boom!
The Giant's footsteps rang in the little tailor's ears. Terrified, he jumped into a small boat and rowed frantically across the lake.

But the little tailor hadn't forgotten the princess's lovely smile. On the opposite shore, he gathered his courage and approached the Giant. The Giant was resting on the roof of a house, as if it were an ordinary stool. The little tailor hid in a cart full of pumpkins, hoping to find a way to take him prisoner.

"He's so big," thought the discouraged tailor, "so strong — so scary."

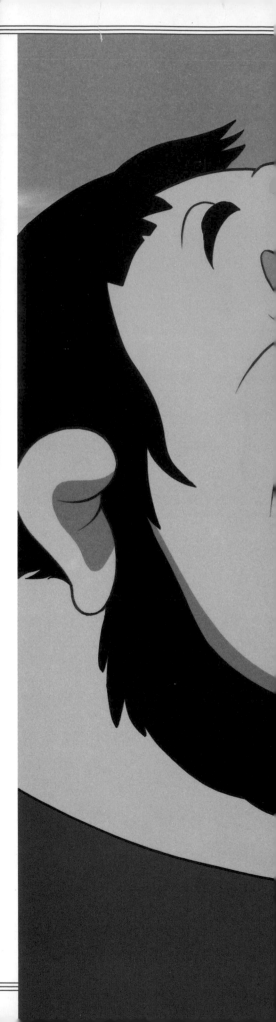

The little tailor had been
distracted and hadn't seen danger
coming. An enormous hand plunged
into the cart where he'd been
hiding. Grabbing a fistful of
pumpkins, the Giant scooped up
the little tailor along with them. The
terrified tailor saw the huge mouth
open, ready to engulf him. The
Giant still wasn't aware of his
existence. Then he threw the tailor
into his mouth with the pumpkins!

Fortunately, the little tailor managed to cling to a tooth. But he wasn't safe yet. Now the Giant wanted a drink and had spotted something that would quench his thirst — a well! He pulled it roughly from the ground and slurped its contents in a single swallow. An immense wave swept the little tailor away.

"Brr! Is it ever dark in here!"

This time the little tailor found himself right in the Giant's stomach. At the last moment, he'd managed to grab the bucket from the well. "This is dreadful," he thought. "I'll never make it out of here."

Suddenly, the voice of the Giant bellowed, "What's scraping me in there? Oh, it's the rope!" The tailor was yanked out of the Giant's mouth and flew through the air. The Giant hadn't seen him.

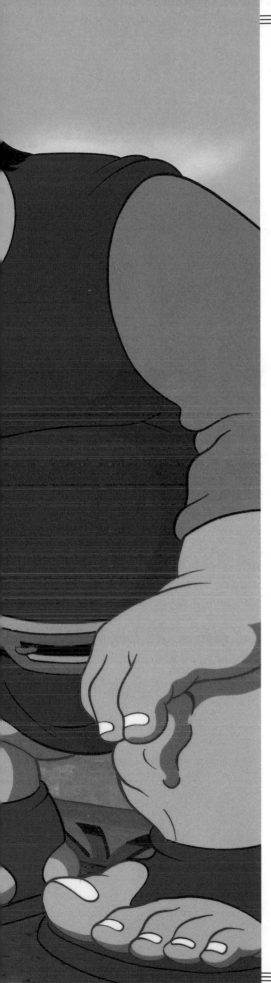

Yet again, the little tailor had escaped. He landed in the straw of a thatched roof without a single scratch! But what was the Giant up to now? Oh, no — he was making a giant toothpick from the thatched roof ... and had rolled the little tailor up inside!

"*At-choo!*" The little tailor sneezed, exploding the toothpick right under the Giant's nose!

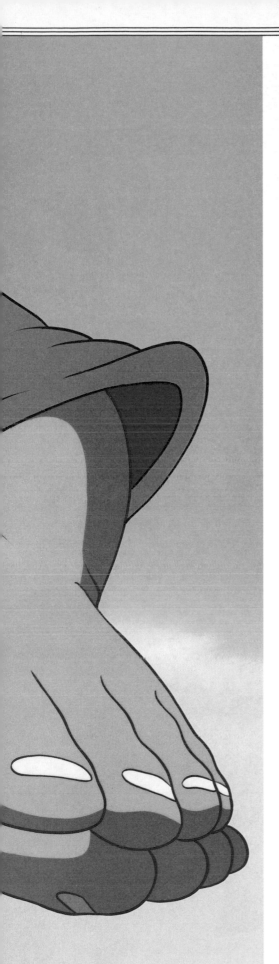

"Who dares disturb me?" yelled the angry giant. "And what kind of mosquito is this?" he added, spotting the little tailor. *Clap! Clap!* He tried to nab Mickey with his hands, but the little tailor was too clever. He crept up into one of the Giant's sleeves, took out his scissors, and — *Snip! Snip!* — cut a hole in the cloth. The Giant tried to capture him with his free hands but the little tailor escaped through the hole he'd made. Now the Giant's arms were pinned.

The little tailor lost no time. Quickly, he slipped an entire spool of thread through his biggest needle and began to bind up the monster. The sleeves were stitched in a couple of minutes, firmly locking in the Giant's arms. Then the little tailor heaved himself onto the Giant's head. "Ow! My nose! Help!" yelped the Giant. But the little tailor, furiously winding his thread, continued to tie him up.

The little tailor had done it! The giant couldn't move. He was bound and trussed like a chicken, pinned down to the ground with stakes.

The little tailor returned to the palace. "Mission accomplished, Your Majesty," he said, bowing respectfully.

The king was astonished. He hadn't really believed that a simple tailor could conquer a giant. But he was so relieved to be rid of the monster that he kept his promise. Next day, the brave little tailor and the princess were married, and a great carnival was held to celebrate the wedding. The Giant would never trouble the kingdom again.

MICKEY

AND THE

BEANSTALK

In a small country, very far away, lived three friends: Goofy, Donald, and Mickey. They were unhappy, for everything was going wrong. The soil was dry and nothing would grow in it, the leafless trees bore no fruit. The hot sun ruled; there had been no rain for months. But the land had been fertile until a stranger had come to the palace and stolen the singing harp that had protected the kingdom and made it rich.

One day, as the three hungry friends were preparing their meager dinner, Goofy said, "What shall we do? Soon there won't be anything to eat."

Mickey had an idea: "Let's sell our cow before she gets too thin. We could use the money to buy food for a few days." Donald wanted to eat the cow for dinner, but Mickey hurried her away to market.

Donald and Goofy stayed home, happily imagining all the delicious food Mickey would bring home for supper.

"I like chicken!" said one.

"And a big cake for dessert!" said the other.

Soon Mickey returned: "I've done it, my friends!" But what was that in his hands? It wasn't a basket full of food, but a strange little box!

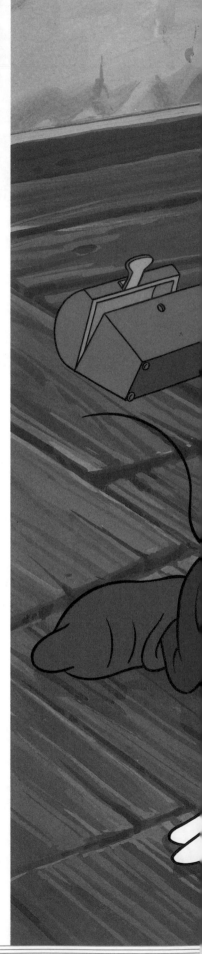

"Guess what happened!" cried Mickey, excited. "I hadn't gone far when I met an old man. He told me that he was a sorcerer, and offered to exchange our cow for this box full of magic beans. He promised they would make us rich!"

"You're crazy; you're making fun of us!" Donald, furious, grabbed the box ... and the beans fell into a crack in the floor.

It was impossible to get the beans back. The friends would never know whether they were really magic, or whether the old man had tricked Mickey.

Everyone went to bed hungry. But while the friends slept, a strange thing happened: a green shoot sprang up from the floor and started to grow and grow. It quickly became a huge beanstalk, which grew through the night and carried the cabin toward the sky.

The three friends woke early the next morning. "Look," cried Mickey, "we're on top of an enormous beanstalk! The seeds *were* magic! One of them grew while we slept and carried us to this place!"

They saw a castle in the distance and decided to pay a visit. On the way, they went through a forest of giant trees. Goofy was fascinated. "Gawrsh!" he said. "I never saw anything so pretty!"

After walking for a long time, they came to a river. To get across, they floated on a leaf that was as big as a boat!

Soon they arrived at the castle. The door was gigantic. They knocked as hard as they could, but the wood was so thick that no one could hear them. Who could live here?

They pushed on the door, and suddenly it opened. And before the astonished friends was a table covered with all the food they'd been dreaming of ... but it was all so big!

Once they had eaten their fill, the three friends explored the castle. They found a chest that seemed to be locked. Curious, Mickey looked through the keyhole.

"Come look," he cried, "I've found the singing harp!"

"Be quiet," she whispered. "This castle belongs to a giant, and he won't be happy if he finds you here!"

"It was he who stole me," the harp added. "But I beg you, don't stay here! It will soon be time for him to eat!"

The harp was right. Suddenly, they heard heavy footsteps. It was the Giant. He put away the ball he'd been playing with and happily sat down to eat.

The three friends hadn't had time to find a good hiding place. The Giant soon found them. "What is this?" he asked in surprise. "This isn't what I usually eat for breakfast!"

His sandwich looked funny, and it talked! "Oh, uh ... hello, Mr. Giant," Mickey stuttered. "Pay me no mind. I'm ... uh, just passing through!" Goofy and Donald also tried to sneak away. But the Giant, furious, caught them all.

To get these pests out of his sight, the Giant threw them into the chest with the singing harp: "There! Now you won't bother me! You, harp! Come with me! You'll sing me a little song while I eat."

While the Giant wolfed down his enormous meal, Mickey managed to escape through the keyhole. But the others were trapped. He had to find the key!

At that moment, a great snoring began. The Giant had eaten too much and, lulled by the singing harp's song, fell into a deep sleep.

"Let's try now!" whispered Mickey.

He slid onto the Giant's shoulder. It took him a long time to find the key in the Giant's pocket. Finally, he grabbed it. Now he had to retrace his steps.

Mickey freed his friends, and the frightened Goofy said, "Quick, let's get out of here! The Giant could wake anytime!"

They lifted the singing harp from the table. "She's too heavy; she'll slow us down," groaned Donald. But they couldn't leave her behind. Without her, their country would never again be prosperous.

With one pushing and one pulling, Donald and Goofy slowly carried the singing harp down the beanstalk. Terrified, she begged them to hurry: "When the Giant sees that I'm gone, he'll be mad with rage. He'll flatten you, I know!"

Mickey looked behind him. There he was! The Giant, club in hand, was in hot pursuit!

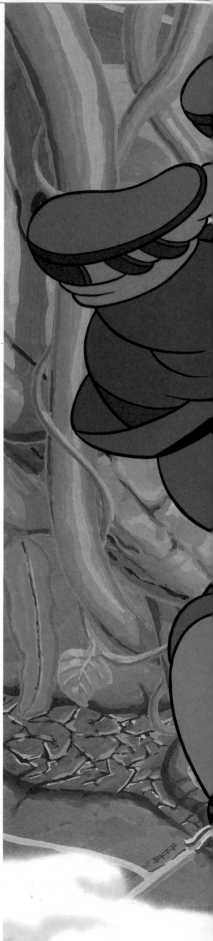

In a great rush, the friends finally reached the ground. They could hear the Giant above them. He was catching up!

"Watch out! Here he comes!" cried Mickey. But Donald and Goofy started to saw at the trunk of the beanstalk.

Finally, the huge plant toppled. Carrying the Giant with it, the beanstalk fell right into a lake, where the monster drowned.

The three friends brought the singing harp to the palace. When they arrived, the harp began to sing. At once, the grass began to grow, and the trees were covered with blossoms.

The king gave the friends marvelous gifts in gratitude. But when he wanted to give a ball in their honor, they refused: "Sire, we must go home to farm our land. Thanks to the singing harp, we know that the kingdom will be prosperous again."

THE COUNTRY COUSIN

Early one spring morning, the country
mouse went fishing in the stream at the
bottom of his field. There he caught a big
trout, which he took home for dinner.

At home, a surprise awaited him: a letter
from his cousin the city mouse, who was
coming to visit the very next day! Happily,
the country mouse prepared the trout for
baking, so that he could serve a fine meal.

Dear country cousin,

I'm planning to come and visit you tomorrow. A day in the country will do me good! I can't wait to see you.

Regards,

Your city cousin

The country mouse cleaned the whole house, and everything was in order when he heard a horn beep outside. Running out to greet his cousin, he exclaimed: "What a handsome car! Did you have a good trip?"

"Yes, indeed," said the city mouse, giving his cousin a hug. He wore a fine suit and a tall top hat and looked very elegant. The cousins talked over family news and sat down to a good dinner. "This is excellent!" said the city mouse. "It's good to have a simple, hearty meal once in a while."

The cousins spent a happy day strolling in the woods and fields. By nightfall, the city mouse was yawning. "This good country air has made me tired!" he exclaimed. So they went to bed under a cozy patchwork quilt.

Before he fell asleep, the city mouse had an idea. "Why should we part tomorrow?" he exclaimed. "We get along so well! Come back to town with me!"

And so the next morning, the two cousins left the peaceful countryside and took the road to town.

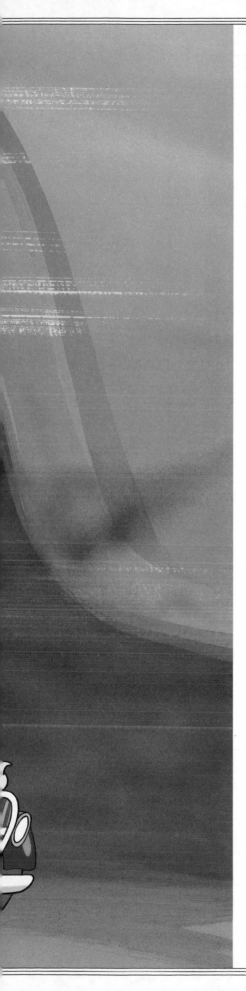

The city mouse was a skillful driver, but he went very fast, and his car was very small! The country mouse trembled whenever a huge car roared past them.

At last the city mouse said, "Here we are in town!"

It's amazing!" cried his passenger. "I've never seen anything like it!"

"And here's my place!" said the city mouse, proud to show off the fancy house to his admiring cousin.

"You never told me you live in a palace!" marvelled the country mouse. "Oh, what a beautiful floor. I can see myself in it."

"Let me show you my room," said the city mouse. "It's my place to relax here in the city."

The country mouse was astonished. "Wow! They put a meal in front of your door?" Hungrily, he approached a piece of cheese.

"Stop!" yelled his cousin, pulling him back just in time. With a nasty *crack*, the trap snapped shut in front of the frightened country mouse. What a narrow escape! The city mouse knew he would have to keep an eye on his country cousin!

"Come on, Cousin! Here's the feast I promised you!" said the city mouse proudly, scurrying onto a high table. The country mouse couldn't believe his eyes. "Are you sure I'm not dreaming?" he asked.

The country mouse didn't know what to eat first. He went from the tasty creampuffs to the giant cheese, then from the sliced ham to the crunchy celery. In the end, he decided to taste everything!

"Hush!" warned his cousin. "Don't make so much noise. We don't want to get caught!"

The country cousin was attracted to something that looked like golden cream. He'd never seen mustard before. He took a big taste. "Ouch! That's hot!" he yelled. Coughing and spluttering, he stuck his head into a glass of cherry soda to cool off!

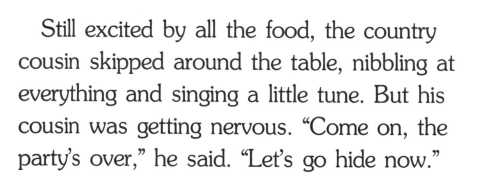

Still excited by all the food, the country cousin skipped around the table, nibbling at everything and singing a little tune. But his cousin was getting nervous. "Come on, the party's over," he said. "Let's go hide now."

Then the country mouse tripped on a plate, which swept the two mice up and slid along the table like a flying saucer. The cousins hung on desperately as the plate zoomed along, knocking over everything in its path. Then it fell from the table with a great *crash!*

Just before the plate dropped, the mice leaped down. The city mouse moaned, "What a racket! It must have awakened the cat!"

He grabbed the country mouse to take him to his hole. But his big foolish cousin said, "If you think that fat city cat scares me ... ha!" Then he shouted, "Here, kitty! Here, little kitty!"

"You'd better watch out!" cried the city mouse, taking shelter when the cat appeared. Then his cousin gave the enormous cat a kick. The cat was furious. With a nasty gleam in his eyes, he turned on the rash rodent.

"Oh! What a big mouth!" The country mouse stared at the cat's long, pointed fangs. But the cat's ferocious growl brought him to his senses. He ran for his life.

The monster, all claws out, pounced — and just missed his prey. Terrified, the country mouse leaped out the window. Luckily, he landed on a roof, then slid down a well-placed gutter. He made it to the ground in one piece. What an adventure!

Thinking the cat was right behind him, the country mouse fled into the night. But the sidewalk was almost as dangerous as the cat had been. People stomped along without noticing him.

"One of those big shoes could crush me," thought the unhappy mouse. "It's a little quieter here. I can catch my breath." But suddenly a screeching, roaring monster arrived: a streetcar!

"Help! I want to go home!" The poor mouse began to cry. Just when he thought he'd found the way, he was almost run over by an enormous limousine! Luckily, he flattened himself on the pavement.

"There's too much traffic! I'll never get home. Unless — I know what to do!" And he started for home following the railroad tracks!

Finally, the tired country mouse got back to his own house. There, all his friends asked eagerly, "Tell us, what's it like in the city?"

"It's big, it's busy, it's amazing," he answered. "But I'm happier in the country ... where it's quiet!"

MICKEY'S CHRISTMAS CAROL

It was Christmas Eve, and
the streets had a festive air.
The townsfolk were in a cheery
holiday mood. Well, not
everyone was in a holiday
mood. Who was that, muttering
so crossly? It was Ebenezer
Scrooge, a rich banker, and the
most miserly man in town.

"Humph! They never think of
work, just amusing themselves,"
he grumbled.

Scrooge was still grumbling when he arrived at his office. "Then they come bothering me for loans. Hmmm... let's see what my clerk is up to. I'll bet he's been slacking off while I've been out. What are you doing, Cratchit? Putting more coal in the stove? You'll be the ruin of me!"

Bob Cratchit was the bank's sole employee since Marley, Scrooge's former partner, had died. He was paid a miserable pittance, and often worked until dark, while his employer counted the gold he had amassed during the day.

"Here's some work," growled Scrooge, slapping an enormous ledger on Cratchit's desk. "That should warm you up!"

When evening came, Cratchit shyly approached his employer. "If you please, sir, could I leave a little early? It's Christmas Eve, and..."

"What? It's only seven o'clock," snapped Scrooge. "Have you finished your work?"

"Why, yes, sir..."

"Hmmm... Well, all right," Scrooge said grudgingly, "but take my laundry to be washed. And make sure you come in early the day after tomorrow."

Scrooge went home in the dark to the house he had shared with Marley. On his way up the stairs he heard strange sounds. Then a shadowy form appeared. He froze in his tracks. It was Marley's ghost!

"Wh-what are you doing here?" Scrooge stammered.

"I come to warn you to change your ways," the ghost replied. "This night three spirits will visit you. Listen well to them. If not, you will end up like me... doomed!"

Then the ghost vanished. Scrooge was frightened. He went to bed, wondering if it had been a dream. He did not want to have any more ghosts visiting him.

He was almost asleep when a little voice said, "I am the Spirit of Christmas Past. Get up, Scrooge. You must come with me."

Scrooge protested, but the ghost silenced him. "Don't ask questions. Catch hold of my coattails, for we are going back in time." And they flew away over the rooftops.

They came to a house. Through the window, Scrooge saw himself when he was younger, with his fiancée. In another scene he saw her crying and wondered why. Then he remembered...

"Your greed destroyed her love, Scrooge," the ghost reminded him.

The Spirit of Christmas Past vanished, leaving Scrooge alone.

Next Scrooge found himself in another place — a room piled high with food, where a giant was eyeing him. He tried to hide, but an enormous hand seized him, and the giant roared, "So this is the rogue, the heartless banker! I am the Spirit of Christmas Present, and I want to show you something."

In a twinkling, Scrooge was again before a window. This time it was Cratchit's house. Tiny Tim, the youngest child, was hobbling with a crutch to join the rest of the family at the table. "Why is the boy so sickly?" Scrooge wondered. As he watched, he became more and more ashamed. "They have practically nothing to eat!" he exclaimed.

The scene was a revelation to Scrooge. "I didn't know that Cratchit was so poor," he sighed.

A scathing voice behind him said, "You might have known! How could he afford a feast for his family with the paltry pay you give him?"

Scrooge turned around. A horrible spirit, its face in shadow, stood before him: the Spirit of Christmas Yet to Come.

Suddenly the scene changed again. Scrooge was in a cemetery. The spectre raised a hand and pointed. Scrooge looked and saw Cratchit and his family with tears on their faces, standing beside Tiny Tim's grave.

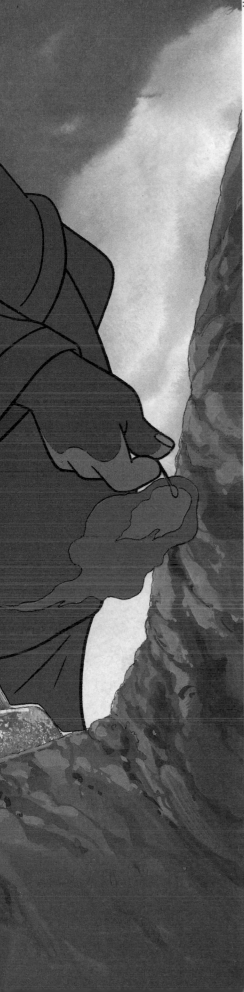

The Spirit of Christmas Yet to Come loomed over Scrooge. "The child's death is your doing. His father could never afford the care he needed. Your greed and meanness have been the cause of much hardship. Now you will pay for your misdeeds. Here is your grave." And the spectre pushed him in...

"No! No!" screamed Scrooge. "I've learned my lesson! I'll change!" A deafening noise was his answer.

Ding, dong! Ding, dong! Scrooge carefully opened his eyes and found himself in his own bed. The bells were ringing on Christmas morning. It had all been a terrible nightmare.

"Hooray! I'm alive!" he shouted. "But that means Tiny Tim is alive, too! He threw on a coat over his nightshirt and ran outside, to the astonishment of his neighbors.

"What has come over him?" people asked each other. They could hardly believe their eyes. Particularly when he pressed gold coins into their hands, saying to everyone, "Merry Christmas! Merry Christmas to all!"

He met his nephew, who had never seen him so cheerful, and told him, laughing, "You see, anyone can change. I'm coming for Christmas dinner at your house tonight. We'll celebrate. But there's one thing I have to do first."

Leaving his nephew speechless, he went to Cratchit's house with a big sack on his back. He put on his grumpy face and knocked. When Cratchit opened the door, his face fell. "You forgot my laundry," said Scrooge, dumping the sack.

"Oh, look," cried Tiny Tim, "there's a teddy bear in Mr. Scrooge's pocket!"

And when the sack was opened, instead of dirty laundry there were presents for the children and an enormous goose and other good things for dinner.

Already overcome with surprise, Cratchit heard Scrooge say, "Tiny Tim must have everything he needs. Tomorrow you will become my new partner. You will never be poor again."

This edition published by
Brimar Publications Inc.
338 Saint-Antoine St. E.
Montreal, Canada H2Y 1A3
Tel. (514) 954-1441
Fax (514) 954-1443

Produced by
Twin Books
15 Sherwood Place
Greenwich, CT 06830
USA

ISBN 2-920845-58-6

Printed in Canada